the girl next door

emma bray

one

· · ·

Addy

I'm painting a little bluebird. He's been coming to visit me every day for a week now.

I mix the colors on my palette, trying to capture his various shades of blue.

He's a pretty bird. I know he's a he because his feathers are so bright and beautiful. Funny how the males always have the prettiest plumage. The females pale in comparison.

I stroke the brush across the canvas, enjoying the smooth glide of the wet paint over the slightly textured surface. I've been painting for as long as I can remember. Ever since I was a little girl, and my dad locked me up in here. I have a TV, although I've never really cared for watching it. And Dad has supplied me with plenty of books.

But painting has always been my favorite thing of all. Time passes quickly when I lose myself in the brushstrokes. I'll start painting in the morning, and before I know it, night has fallen. I don't notice the sun setting until it's already disappeared beyond the horizon. That's what I love about painting. I can lose myself completely in the creation emerging on the canvas. Forget that I'm a pretty bird in a gilded cage.

I paint birds more than anything else because I feel like one, only I'm trapped. I long to spread my wings like the birds that swoop and soar through the sky just outside my window. I wish I could capture one and bring it in here with me, keep it as a pet so I won't be so lonely.

But then I remember what it's like to be locked up in this room, and I could never subject one of those precious creatures to the same fate.

Sometimes, I paint them in cages with intricate ironwork. But no matter how pretty I make the cage, they're so much prettier painted soaring free through the sky.

My room is beautiful, large and tastefully decorated with its own luxurious bathroom.

I remember the last time I left this room. It was the

day I turned fourteen. My father never forgets my birthday, but we never celebrate it either because it marks the day my mother died. Dad chooses to remember that instead, that she died giving birth to me.

You killed your mother. That's what he told me. And, honestly, I get it. How can he celebrate the birth of the person who killed his wife?

The guilt is constant. I wish I could've known her. But that's one of life's great ironies because she'd still be here if not for me. But it is what it is. I can't change any of it.

The day I turned fourteen, Dad had a bunch of his business associates over for dinner. Until that point, I had free run of the house. I was able to go to the library, the kitchen, and the backyard, which was completely fenced in. Sure, the fence was too high to see over, and no one could see in, but at least I was able to smell the grass and feel the breeze on my skin.

That was four years ago

Four long years.

I still cringe when I remember that fateful birthday when everything changed.

I wanted to make Dad proud. I wanted to show him that I supported him and that I was growing up to be responsible. So, I brushed out my long, caramel-colored hair and put on my prettiest white dress and went down to the dinner. Uninvited.

Dad never explicitly told me to stay out of sight when his business associates were over, but it was like an unspoken order. I stayed away when he had company and left him to his business.

Never before had I dared to let myself be seen.

But for some reason, I did that day.

I walked into the dining room, where Dad was seated at the head of the table. Every other chair was occupied with men my dad's age and older. There must have been at least twenty of them in the room with my father.

The conversation ceased when I entered the room, and every gaze turned on me. There was something unsettling in each of the men's eyes that I still don't understand, but the memory still makes me shiver to this day.

At first, Dad seemed furious at my interruption, but when he saw the attention I was receiving, he invited me to sit down right next to him. My heart soared and I smiled. I was happy to be sitting next to him like I was important. Like he was proud of me.

Several men spoke to me and told me how pretty I was. They asked Dad where he'd been hiding me all this time. He merely smiled and didn't answer.

After everyone left, I was beaming, glad to have

been accepted by my father. I was hoping I could hug him. I could count on one hand the times my father had hugged me.

Twice. It was exactly twice.

I wanted a hug more than anything else in the world. From my dad.

But when everyone was gone, he sternly ordered me to my room.

I didn't protest, although I was confused. I just obeyed.

I heard the lock turn from the outside. Funny. I'd never really noticed my room had a lock before.

I haven't been outside this room since that day.

No amount of crying or begging or pleading or asking what I'd done would convince my father to free me. He's the type of man who doesn't owe anyone any explanations, so he's certainly never offered me any.

My dad's cook brings me food every day. I stopped trying to talk to him after my first year in here. I don't even know his name. He never responded to me when I asked him, so I just call him "Cook" in my mind. He never speaks to me. I don't know if it's because he's cold and unfeeling or if my dad has ordered him not to. I like to believe it's the latter. I've never thought my dad was a bad father. He's never hit me or raised his voice to me. He's never shown me any affection either. The few times he's spoken to me, it was to explain why

I couldn't have a birthday party. That I'd killed my mother. He stated it matter-of-factly, and that was that.

Then, he went back to ignoring me.

I've never been allowed out of the house other than in that small fenced-in area of the backyard. We live right on the ocean, but I've never felt the sand in my toes or the water washing over my feet.

I've never been to school. Dad has me do some self-guided online learning, but my computer is locked down, so I don't have access to social media or the net. There's no way for me to communicate with the outside world, although it's not like I have friends, anyway. Unless I count the characters from my books.

My father's not cruel to me. He supplies me with everything I ask for as long it's nothing to do with the internet or communication. I have all the clothes, books, paint supplies, and puzzles my heart desires. He gives me what he can, I suppose.

When I get down and depressed and feel like a captive, I remind myself how good I have it. I've read plenty of books about captives, and I know that most of them don't have the luxuries I do. Plus, I'm here with my own father, so it's not like he's kidnapped me or anything. I tell myself that he has a good reason for doing what he does, that he's noble and trying to protect me.

I don't always believe that, but I can pretend.

I may not be able to leave this cage, but at least it's a pretty one, and I can have almost anything I want to keep myself occupied. Just not the one thing I really want. Someone, anyone to take away my loneliness.

I don't know why he's kept me locked away. I've always assumed it was out of shame for the daughter who killed his wife by being born.

I feel a lump rise in my throat as I think about it for the millionth time. I committed matricide the day I was born.

And I guess being locked away like this is my punishment.

———

Alec

I'm standing on the balcony of my grandfather's house —well, it's my house now, but I still think of it as his.

I never thought I would be back here in my hometown, the city where I grew up. When I left L.A, I went as far away as I could— to the other side of the country, to be exact. I settled in New York, and I haven't looked back. It's not that I have anything against the place where I grew up, per se. There was just nothing keeping me here.

There's not much love lost between me and the

grandfather who raised me. We didn't necessarily have a contentious relationship, but he was no substitute for a much-needed father figure. Rather, he was just an old man doing his duty. And I suppose I'm grateful for that now.

I don't know why I was surprised when he left his house to me. He didn't have anyone else to leave it to.

I still have my apartment in New York but there's nothing keeping me there either. My business ventures have been so successful I can live anywhere I want now.

I honestly don't know if I'm going to sell this house or not. I figured I needed to come back and see the old place before making my decision. I don't have particularly fond memories of my youth here, but I don't have traumatic ones either.

It's simply the place where I grew up.

I look out over the ocean, watching as the last of the sun's rays glisten over the waves of the Pacific in a glorious display of pinks, purples, and oranges. How did I forget this beautiful view? It might be worth keeping for that alone. Of course, this view will also be a major selling point if I decide to list it.

Love it or list it. Isn't that the name of some HGTV show? I don't watch much TV, preferring to keep my mind occupied with work, but it sounds familiar.

My eyes are drawn to the mansion next door. My

grandfather's house is nothing to sniff at, but it doesn't compare to the luxury that sits next door. I remember it from growing up here, though I've never been over there. As far as I know, a widower lives there all alone —at least that's what I've always heard.

Several of the rooms are lit up, but my gaze is pulled to the glow at the top of the house. The house has a turret like a medieval castle, although the style is anything but outdated. It's modern and tastefully done, a feat in contemporary architecture.

I can see right inside the window. There's an easel with a canvas propped up on it. Huh. Who'd have thought the old widower was a painter? I wonder if he's any good or if he's just one of those who dabbles in it just to give himself something to do.

As I turn to go back inside the comfort of the house, a movement catches my eye in the window.

My mouth goes dry, and my heart thunders in my ears when I see a girl's figure move into sight.

I don't know why I'm so arrested by her, but it's as if my world has imploded right in front of my eyes. Something about her captivates me, making it impossible to look away from her.

She's breathtakingly gorgeous. And Christ Almighty, all she has on is a white bra and panty set, though it's thinly veiled with a white button-up shirt that she's left to hang open like a robe.

She's thin, but I can see the gentle curves of her body. Light brown hair cascades down her back to her waist. She's turned toward the canvas, so I'm looking at her profile. It keeps me from seeing her eyes, and I'm suddenly desperate to know what color they are.

She picks up a brush and a paint palette and starts to paint.

I watch the gentle sway of her body as she holds the palette in one hand and strokes the canvas with the other. She paints swiftly, her brush frequently mixing the paints squirted on the palette she's holding in her hand.

Who is she? Somehow, I can't see her being the old man's wife. She looks too young. His daughter, perhaps? But if he has a daughter, how come I never saw her at school? Was she homeschooled? I know I've never seen her before because there's no way I'd forget the vision standing in that window.

I stare at her in fascination. I'm not sure how long I stand there, but by the time her shoulders finally sag in exhaustion, and she lays down her brush and palette, the sun has descended over the ocean.

She finally turns and looks out the window.

And directly into my eyes.

Her eyes are more stunning than I could have imagined. A rich honey-colored caramel. They gaze right into mine, widening for a fraction of a second when she realizes I've been watching her.

Most women would probably pull their shirt tighter around themselves and retreat out of view, but she doesn't.

No, she steps right up to the window and curls her fingers against the glass.

As if she's reaching out to me, trying to touch me.

As if she's as entranced by me as I am her.

It's a move that would seem forward coming from any other woman, but somehow, with her, it's just… not. If anything, it makes her seem even more innocent. It's not that she isn't sexy because she is, but there's a sinful innocence about her that grips and claws at a man until all he wants is one taste.

She may be scantily clad and standing in front of her window for me to see, but she doesn't come across as calculating or flirty.

She's purity. Innocence personified. A vision.

Her lips are unsmiling, but they're not frowning either. They're full and pink and perfect.

As if she can sense the direction of my thoughts, she licks them and bites down on the bottom one.

My blood roars in my ears as the lower half of my body reacts and my blood heads south.

Holy mother of God, has this girl been next door all this time? Why have I never seen her before?

The questions burn in my mind, and I've halfway decided to go over there and introduce myself, demand to know who she is, when she suddenly turns, and I see her lips moving.

Someone's in the room with her. I keep watching her profile and frown as I see her shrink in on herself, her shoulders curling up.

Anger flares in my chest, hot and heavy. The sudden wave of protectiveness for her should startle me, but it doesn't. Instead, the need to know who's eliciting that kind of reaction from her consumes me.

I never find out because a moment later, the room goes dark.

I continue to stare up at the turret, wondering if she'll come back to the window to say goodnight.

I shake my head when I realize the direction my thoughts have taken. Say goodnight?

I inhale deeply and run a hand through my hair before I blow it back out, chancing one last look up at the window.

Empty. The way my chest suddenly feels.

I can't fully explain the way my stomach drops at the thought that she's not coming back tonight.

I don't even know her name.

But I decide right then and there that I will soon.

two

· · ·

Addy

I lay in the dark and ponder the night's strange occurrences.

The man I saw standing on the balcony. His dark hair and startling green eyes that remind me of grassy fields or the forest. They were so green and full of life. He was tall and broad-shouldered, standing there all alone and staring right at me.

How long has it been since anyone saw me? *Really* saw me?

He was staring into my eyes so intensely it took my breath away. I haven't had eye contact like that in so long—if ever.

His eyes…they looked like freedom.

And he was beautiful. I couldn't do anything but stare back at him, feeling more alive than I've ever felt.

My skin vibrated and flushed. There was a sudden pulse between my thighs, an ache that confused me but had me biting my lip.

I wanted to reach out and touch him, lose myself in the forest of his eyes.

But then I heard the lock turn, snapping my focus from the beautiful man on the balcony to the door behind me.

Dad rarely visits me, so I was surprised to see his tall frame filling the doorway. His eyes swept over me with disdain before he barked at me to "put some clothes on, for Christ's sake."

In my defense, no one ever comes up here except Cook, and that's only to provide meals. Still, I hated hearing that tone from my father and couldn't help the slump of my shoulders. Nothing I do has ever made him happy.

And why would it? A little voice inside my head whispered to me. *You killed his wife. He told you so himself.*

I stood there nervously, waiting to see what he wanted. He never visits me without reason.

I was shocked when he didn't say another word to me. He just walked over to my closet and began rifling through my hangers, muttering to himself. I watched him warily, wondering at his strange behavior. If I was hoping for an explanation, I was sadly disappointed when he finally turned on his heel and headed out the door without another word or glance.

I turned off the light and went straight to bed, but I can't sleep. All I can do is wonder at my father's strange actions while my mind keeps pulling me back to the man next door.

My skin heats again as I remember the way the wind tousled his dark hair. I feel the incessant throbbing between my legs and tentatively move my fingers down there. I've read some romance novels that were probably my mother's. Any time I asked for books, Dad had a bunch sent up from the library. I'm sure he didn't select them himself. Cook probably grabbed a box and lugged them up here without checking what he was giving me. So, I know the semantics of sex. I know what a man and woman are supposed to do, and I know that a woman can get pleasure from climaxing.

I just don't know how to do it.

I've tried touching myself before like the heroines in some of the books do, but I can't ever seem to reach that pinnacle they talk about.

I try now, stroking my fingers across my pearly nub. I feel snaps of pleasure shooting up from that bundle of nerves. I think of the beautiful man next door, imagining him as one of the heroes from the romance novels, and I feel myself becoming wetter.

There's something just beyond my reach. I keep climbing and climbing, but I can't reach that summit.

I huff in frustration, and just like all the other times, I finally give up.

And lay there with that ache still in between my legs until I finally drift off.

The last thing I see in my mind before I succumb to sleep are piercing green eyes.

And I dream of flying through the forest.

Far away from here and this house.

———

Alec

Addison Jameson.

That's her name.

It didn't take my investigator long to pull up that Donald Jameson, my next-door neighbor, has a daughter, but other than she got her GED online, there isn't much to know. There aren't any school records of her, no social media profiles, no hospital records other than her birth.

Nothing.

It's like she's never existed in the outside world.

I also had my guy do some digging on Donald for good measure. I never really knew much about the widower next door, other than he was some sort of successful businessman. He'd have to be to have the kind of estate he does.

However, my investigator's probing found disturbing evidence that the old man's business dealings are not on the up and up. He's connected to some powerful men who are known for unscrupulous practices, men who may be tied to the criminal underworld.

I have my suspicions about him, so I know that wherever this leads, I'll have to tread carefully.

I sit inside my bedroom and stare up at Addison's window. The view isn't as good from here as it is from the balcony. I'm viewing it at an angle, but it allows me to watch her surreptitiously.

"Addison." I speak her name aloud, almost reverently, loving the way it rolls off my tongue. It suits her.

She's painting again. This time she's sitting on a stool, and she's wearing more clothing than she was last night—though not much. Short shorts and a thin tank top. Her long hair flows down her back, bouncing lightly with her brushstrokes.

She's exquisite.

Sometimes she just stops and gazes ahead of her, looking off into the ocean. A quick survey of the house told me that she's also got windows on the other side of her room facing the Pacific. She sits there for minutes at a time with the saddest look on her face.

She looks out of that window longingly like she's trapped.

And I start to wonder if she is.

I mean, I grew up in this house, and I never saw a girl. I'm twenty-eight, and she looks to be in her teens, so wouldn't I have seen a little girl over there?

The longer I stare at her sad face, the more I become convinced that she's a captive, a pretty bird in a gilded cage. I don't know how I know. I just *know*.

And I want to know why. I want to rescue her. I want to be her savior.

I sit there all day and watch her. She paints. She stares morosely out the window with her knees pulled up to her chin. She reads.

But she's always in front of the window as if she craves the sunlight and is trying to absorb whatever she can through the glass.

When I see a tear trickle down her cheek, my heart wrenches within my chest.

I can't take it anymore and make my way out onto the balcony.

I need to let her know she's not alone. That I see her, and I care. That I want to help her.

She wipes her face and stands up as soon as I step

out onto the balcony, moving closer to the window until she's damn near pressed up against it.

My heart rate picks up in my chest as I take in her shapely legs and ivory skin. She's like a princess in a tower, and I'm the prince who's finally come to release her.

Her caramel eyes are pinned on me, and all I can do is gaze back at her.

She's so breathtakingly beautiful.

When I finally get my wits about me, I motion for her to open her window.

She looks down and shakes her head sadly, showing me that it won't open.

My blood roars in my ears with a mixture of excitement and fury that my suspicions are proving correct.

She *is* a prisoner.

I hold my fingers up in a calling motion, trying to ask her if there's a way I can call her.

She shakes her head again sadly.

I stare at her, contemplating my next move. I don't know how to communicate with her from here.

But then she smiles at me, a radiant smile that makes her even more beautiful.

My god, she is purity itself with that smile.

I smile back at her, and her cheeks turn pink.

She presses her hand against the glass, and somehow, I know what she's trying to say. We don't even need words. It's like I can feel her soul tethering to mine across the divide between us.

She's sharing herself with me wordlessly, trusting me with the shine of her eyes and the grace of her smile.

And at that moment, I know I'm going to save her. I don't know what her story is, but I'm going to find out, and when I do, I'm going to make her mine.

three

. . .

Alec

I've studied the house next door and everything I could find out about Donald Jameson for a week straight. The security is tight as a motherfucker over there, and I finally realize the only way I'm going to get in is to pretend to want to go into business with the old man.

That's why I'm now sitting in Donald Jameson's study, trying to remain cool and composed. It seems that Donald is one of those men with his hands in everything. He can't get enough and is always willing to branch out. My portfolio was sufficiently impressive to get me a meeting with him.

To get me inside his house.

Where his daughter is locked up upstairs.

I've sat with her every night this week. She sits in her window, and I sit on my balcony, and we just stare at each other, communicating with our eyes. The smile that lights up her face and melts the caramels of her eyes tells me just how grateful she is to have my company, as silent as it is.

My heart breaks for the girl, imagining her so alone that simply having a man sit outside on his balcony and stare at her can make her so happy.

I've considered climbing up the fucking wall and smashing in her window to break her free, but Jameson has too many cameras for that.

I'd be shot in a second.

So, despite every cell in my body screaming at me to run up there, knock down her door, and whisk her away from here, the rational part of my brain is telling me that's not a good idea. That this is going to be much more difficult than simply taking her.

Donald has her locked away for a reason, and I'm starting to figure out why.

So far, he's casually asked me if I'm married or dating. Once he discovered I wasn't, he subtly mentioned his daughter, turning his body slightly to allow me to see the picture of her all dolled up in a white dress looking pure and sweet and virginal.

"She's a good girl," he drawls. "Sweet and obedient. Innocent." He pauses over the last word, glancing at me knowingly.

I keep my expression apathetic, giving nothing away. "Is that so?" He studies me for a moment longer, trying to get a read on me, no doubt.

I give him nothing. I'd hate myself forever if I objectified Addison that way, but I can't show my derision outright and spook him. So, I play the indomitable businessman. Detached yet not disinterested.

The man couldn't be more obvious if he came right out and said it. He's bartering his daughter like a bargaining chip. Using her to further his business endeavors. And I'm practically seething as I wonder how many other fuckers he's made these insinuations to.

"How can you ensure her innocence?" I hate myself for the question, but I have to give him something. I need to know for certain what he's got going on here.

His eyes light up at my interest. "Trust me, she is. The girl hasn't been out of her room since she was fourteen. She's pure."

I run a thumb along my lip thoughtfully and raise an eyebrow at him. "So, you just locked her up in her room for…how old is she now?"

"Eighteen," he assures me before he chuckles to himself. "And consider it a modern-day chastity belt. It wasn't that hard. She's an amicable girl, my daughter. Submissive, obedient, willing to please."

The way he refers to his own daughter so callously has me clenching my fists, but I force myself to relax.

"When can I meet her?" I try to keep my voice impassive like it's no big deal to me either way.

Donald has an unsettling twinkle in his eye. "Let's not get ahead of ourselves, my boy. I have plenty of other business associates interested in her, too." He chuckles to himself again. I want to punch the fucker's lights out.

Calm, I tell myself. *Stay calm. You can't help her if you're dead or in jail.*

Oh, yes, I already know from my research that this fucker has the local police force deep in his pockets. There won't be any 911 calls to get Addison freed. This man is more crooked than I ever anticipated.

Therefore, I have to be patient and go about this the smart way.

I shrug like his daughter is no big deal to me, and I see a moment of panic flare in the old man's eyes. Yes, I've also done some digging on his other business associates, and I know I'm the one packing the most potential. Jameson knows it, too. He's playing hard to get, but he already knows he wants my business—at whatever cost, even at the cost of his own flesh and blood.

"However, I'm planning a dinner party this weekend with all my associates," he rushes to divulge. "Addison will be the guest of honor. Everyone will have a chance to meet her."

"And, let me guess, whoever offers you the best deal gets her?" I ask him, my voice level.

He narrows his eyes at me. "Certain negotiations will have to be made, of course. She *is* my only daughter, Garison."

I try not to grit my teeth at the old man's casual use of my last name. "Naturally," I cock my head and raise my brandy snifter at him, conceding his point–or so he thinks.

He sits back in his chair, mollified for the time being, and pulls out a cigar. He offers me one, but I politely decline.

I've never been one for smoking.

However, I accept another drink when he offers it, even though I haven't finished the one I have. I'm studiously taking small sips to look like I'm drinking. On the other hand, Jameson gulps down his liquor like there's no tomorrow. And that's perfect for what I have planned.

I shoot the shit with him for another hour and watch as the man goes through four more glasses of brandy, becoming more inebriated by the second.

I put on an act of loosening up as well, although I'm far from intoxicated.

I laugh at his crude jokes and talk numbers with him.

Once I sense his guard is down, I ask him where I can take a piss.

He motions sloppily toward the door. "Three doors down on the right," he slurs, taking another sip.

Fucking drunk.

I get up and turn in the direction he motioned, but instead of heading down the hallway, I make my way stealthily toward the stairs.

I'm under no illusions that I'll be able to bust her out of here tonight, but that doesn't mean I can't finally talk to her and let her know that everything's going to be okay.

———

Addy

I jump when I hear someone rattling the doorknob, staring at it like it's a deadly spider. Cook and Dad never jiggle the knob. They've got a key, so their entry is always smooth. A faint knock and the hushed yet urgent whisper of my name have me tiptoeing to the door.

"Addison!" a deep, masculine voice hisses my name through the door.

I melt. Something about that voice makes me feel so *safe*. Safe and wanted and carefree.

A spark of joy and excitement bubbles up from deep within me. Someone knows my name. Someone wants to talk to me!

I rush over to the door and follow his lead to be discreet.

"Yes?" I stage whisper just loud enough to be heard but not so loud that I'm using my full-on speaking voice.

"Oh, thank God." He instantly sounds relieved. "Listen, sweetheart. I'm Alec, the man from next door."

My heart jumps into my throat when I picture his forest-green eyes and dark hair. I've tried to capture those eyes on the canvas all week. I keep painting forests over and over again like a woman possessed, but I still don't feel like I'm getting it quite right. I need to look right into his eyes up close…

I flatten my palm against the door as I repeat his name. "Alec…"

Something like a tortured groan sounds from the other side of the door.

"Call me Addy. My friends call me Addy." My cheeks burn when I realize I don't have any friends.

Thankfully, he doesn't comment on that or make me feel stupid. Instead, he just repeats my nickname.

"Addy." The way he says my name has me whimpering and clenching my thighs together where I sit pressed against the door.

"What are you doing here?" I'm confused and curious but happy all the same. This man has been keeping me silent company for the past week. He sits there and lets me stare at him, and he stares back at me with little hand signals and smiles. They're *our* smiles. Our secret smiles that we use to communicate without words. He tells me, *I'm here. It's okay.* He's been the light in my captivity.

My only friend. The only one who sees me.

"Look, I have to go, sweetheart. I can't explain everything now, but here. Take this."

I stare in amazement as a piece of paper slides under the doorway.

He waits for me to pull it the rest of the way through before he speaks again.

"I'll be back for you, Addy. Just be brave and wait for me, sweet girl," he reassures me.

"Do you promise?" I whisper, biting my lip, needing the confirmation. God, now that I've met him, I can't bear the thought of him leaving me, forgetting me.

"I promise, sweetheart."

There's a moment of silence during which I just

know his hand is splayed against the other side of the door right against mine, nothing but the wood separating our palms.

And then I register the soft beats of his footsteps retreating down the hall.

Intense loss overwhelms me, but then I remember the note. I open it, my eyes greedily reading the contents like they're my lifeline.

I see you. You're not alone.

Two simple lines, but my heart soars and threatens to burst from my body. He's thoughtful, too. He's left no name, nothing to indicate that this isn't something I've scribbled myself in case my father finds it. Nothing to get me in trouble if this scrap of paper is discovered. Yet, he's reassured me that everything I've seen in his eyes over the last week is real.

I press the note against my chest, tears glistening in my eyes. I'm overflowing with so many emotions. Thankfulness, tenderness, longing, but most of all, hope.

I want to give him something in return.

I pick myself up off the floor and sit in my window to wait for him, my heart serene and full of trust for this man I barely know yet who's quickly become the most important thing in my life.

four

. . .

Alec

When I finally make my way back home and out onto the balcony, Addy is waiting for me.

She's standing in her window looking too damn pretty for words. She smiles at me and presses her hand against the glass in that way she always does.

How I want to break that glass right now and set her free, but I restrain myself.

She's wearing a light pink, silky gown. It comes to mid-thigh, and the straps on her shoulders are so thin it's almost like they're not there. It's a simple sleep outfit, not overly sexy, but on her, it looks like straight sugar. Her hair cascades down her back and around her shoulders, encasing her in a sheen of silky, honey-colored strands.

She looks delectable.

I smile at her and give her my customary wave and nod of acknowledgment before I rest my forearms casually on the balcony and continue to stare at her.

God, will I ever be able to look at her enough? I can sit here all day, drinking in just the sight of her and still yearn for more.

She bites her lip nervously as she continues to look at me. Her eyes flicker with uncertainty, but then her fingers move to the straps of her negligee and begin easing them down her shoulders.

My eyes widen, and my cock instantly hardens, pressing right up against the zipper of my slacks. I watch in amazement, scared to blink in case this is a hallucination. I don't want to lose this vision.

I stand, my fingers gripping the rail of the balcony so hard I'm surprised I don't shatter it.

Smooth, creamy skin starts coming into view, inch by precious inch, revealing the gentle swell of her breasts until I'm dying with anticipation.

She pauses for a moment, holding the garment clutched against her chest as her eyes seek out mine.

I stare right into her eyes, communicating that she's okay. She doesn't have to do anything she doesn't want to, but fuck if I'm not dying for more.

She bites her lip again and then takes a shaky breath before she moves her hands to her sides, releasing the fabric.

It glides down over her breasts, her taut stomach, and the gentle swell of her hips before falling to a silky pool at her feet.

She stands in the window completely naked, the warm lamplight illuminating her like an ethereal fairy.

The rosebuds of her nipples are pink and tight, and my greedy eyes trail down over a perfectly flat stomach to the apex of her thighs, where the most perfect little mound I've ever seen sits innocently.

Fucking hell. My cock begins to leak, staining the inside of my pants, and I grip it tightly to keep from ejaculating all over myself like a horny teenager.

Her eyes widen when she sees me grip myself, and she licks those luscious lips of hers again. I can see them shimmering with wetness all the way over here, and I can't stop the guttural groan that leaves me at the thought of tasting her sweetness.

I want to lick and suck every sweet inch of her skin. There's no torture like having her sweet body completely bared to me yet separated by this huge chasm.

But I recognize this for what it is. This sweet, horny little virgin trusts me. She's giving herself to me, showing me a part of herself she's never shown anyone else.

She splays her hand out on her window again in supplication.

I know what she wants, and I could never deny my sweet girl anything. My heart feels like it's about to burst out of my chest. With one yank, I rip my shirt from my body.

If possible, her eyes grow even wider as she drinks me in. I'm tingling just from the heat of her gaze on my skin. I work out every day, and the way she's looking at me in awe right now makes it all worthwhile.

Her eyes trail down my chest, over my stomach, and to my pants before she lifts them back to mine shyly.

Fuck me. I'm about to blow my load right here and now, just from the innocently curious look on her face.

I undo the buckle of my belt slowly, never taking my eyes off her, watching her for any sign of indecision.

But her caramel pools seem to melt with the intense heat of her gaze fastened on my bulge, so I undo my pants, allowing my swollen flesh to spring free.

Her eyes go as wide as saucers, and her pretty little mouth falls open as she stares at me in wonderment.

Christ Almighty, this girl has never seen a cock before, and I'm getting a thrill out of being the first—

and only—one she's ever going to see. Just the thought of another man seeing this look of innocent wonder on her face fills me with rage.

My head of my shaft is glistening with precum. A steady stream of it is trickling down my length, and it's taking all I can do not to stroke myself to the sight before me. Fuck, I don't want to scare her, but I'm going to explode if I don't do something soon.

Addy's chest is moving up and down as her breathing becomes shallower, and then my eyes damn near bug out of my head when she moves a tentative hand down between her legs and begin to rub herself in slow circles.

Fuck!

I can't stop myself. I grip the base of my cock and begin to stroke my dick, keeping pace with her, my eyes glued to her little fingers working her clit.

Christ Almighty, I can see her juices glistening on her fingers.

My breathing becomes more ragged. Fuck, I'm close. So motherfucking close.

But I hold back, unwilling to climax without her. My balls are drawn up so tight it's almost painful.

I drag my gaze back up to her eyes just as she does the same.

Our eyes lock, and we both detonate.

Her mouth falls open in a little "o," and her hair

falls down to kiss her butt as she throws her head back and twitches, her entire body flushing with the force of her orgasm. I see her sweet cream gushing down her thighs, and the picture she paints is too erotic. I couldn't hold back any longer if I wanted to.

My release hits me like a shotgun shell, shattering my body with its potency. Thick ropes tear from my swollen head. Over and over again, I ejaculate, and just when I think I'm done, I keep coming. Fuck, I don't think I've ever come so hard in my entire life.

And all the while, I keep staring straight into her caramel pools as she watches me in blatant amazement.

Her cheeks and throat and chest are flushed. Her legs seem to wobble, and she finally collapses onto her knees, still staring at me through the window.

She places both of her hands on the glass before she leans in and presses her lips against it.

I feel that kiss deep in my soul.

If she wasn't already before, it's now a certain fact.

Addy Jameson is *mine*.

Addy

I'm lying in my bed with Alec's note clutched to my chest again, a soft smile on my face.

I can't believe I finally did it. I finally know the ecstasy talked about in all the romance novels I read.

It's Alec. He's the key I needed to unlock my passion. The way his eyes had burned into mine, kissing my skin with every flick across it, seeing him stroke the pulsing shaft between his legs, knowing that *I* made him that way…it got me hotter than I've ever been before until I was finally able to rise over that crest.

I wonder what it would be like to feel his skin on mine. His body looks big and hard. I can't imagine how the thing between his legs would ever fit inside me, but I'd be willing to try if it made him happy.

I want to be fused to him in every way. I want to share that deep connection with him, to become one person with him.

More than anything, I want to feel his arms around me, just holding me.

Alec would hug me. I know he would.

I stroke my hand over the note still pressed against my chest and allow my heavy lids to close.

Like every other night since I've met him, the last thing I see in my mind before sleep overcomes me are green eyes.

five

. . .

Alec

I keep having "business meetings" with Donald. He thinks I'm eager to lay the groundwork for our "deal," but the truth is I'm doing anything I can to get into his house and get him drunk enough that I can sneak upstairs to speak to Addy again before his big dinner party this weekend.

The dinner party where he's going to parade his daughter around in front of a bunch of wolves like she's the prime rib they have to fight over.

My fists clench, and I take a calming breath as I fight down the urge to jump across his desk and pummel him.

"Just out of curiosity," I ask Jameson with a bored look on my face once he's three drinks in, "what made you decide to lock up your daughter? Couldn't control her otherwise? Was she a wild child or something?"

Jameson chuckles as he shakes his head. "No, nothing like that. Addison's always been obedient to a fault. Never gave me any trouble." He leans toward me conspiratorially and drops his voice a notch as if he's imparting a great secret to me. "No, I locked her up because I knew she was a prize gem. Lock a woman away and call her forbidden fruit and men will suddenly be willing to do anything for a taste."

I take in the man's glassy eyes, and my stomach curdles. This fucker is sick, and I'd gladly kill him with my bare hands if I didn't know his "associates" would come after me—and more importantly, Addy—as soon as word got out.

Jameson, idiot that he is, mistakes the look I didn't mask quickly enough for anticipation or agreement or some shit because he releases a deep, booming laugh as he sits back in his chair. "Don't worry, my boy. You'll get your chance to bid on her tomorrow night, just like everyone else. Just between you and me, I hope you're the one who gets her. I look forward to working with you more."

The fucker has the audacity to wink at me. I go

along with the charade, doing what I have to so I can speak with my sweet girl. "Cheers to that," I lift my brandy glass and watch as Jameson readily takes the bait, knocking down the rest of his drink.

The drunker Jameson gets, the faster he drinks, intoxicating himself even more quickly.

Thirty minutes later, I deem it safe enough to excuse myself to use his restroom.

Like before, I fly swiftly yet quietly up the stairs to Addy's room.

I tap softly on the door before whispering her name. "Addy?"

Just a few seconds later, I hear her overjoyed whisper coming from the other side of the door, "Alec? Is it really you?"

"Yes, sweetheart." My heart warms at the sound of her voice, and my hands twitch with the need to touch her. "Listen, your father's hosting a dinner party with a bunch of his business associates tomorrow night, and he's going to bring you down."

There's a long moment of silence before she finally whispers incredulously, hopefully. "He's letting me out of my room? Will you be there?"

God, the knowledge that she wants me as badly as I want her does something to my insides. My chest feels tight, and while it's a discomforting sensation, I wouldn't trade it for anything in the world if it means Addy desires my presence. "Yes, that's what I wanted to talk to you about, sweetheart. You can't let on that you know me, okay? Don't act happy to see me. Treat me like any of the other men, okay?"

"But why?" she asks me, confused.

My heart wrenches within me. This poor thing has no clue how devious or dangerous her father truly is. Locking some girls away might have made them bitter, but it's only kept Addy painfully childlike in her innocence. This girl has been completely sheltered from everything. And all for a nefarious end game.

"I can't go into it all right now, Addy, but just trust me. Can you do that, sweetheart? I have a plan. I promise you that everything is going to be okay."

She doesn't hesitate before she whispers back fervently. "Yes, of course. I trust you, Alec. I'll do as you say."

"Good girl," I whisper back. "I've got to go now, sweetheart. I'll see you tomorrow night."

"Alec?" she calls tentatively as I turn to leave.

I take a step toward her door again, craning my head down to hear her whisper. "Yes, angel?"

"Can we do what we did that night again?" Her voice is husky with lust and longing.

And just like that, I'm rock hard and biting back a

groan. Fuck, she's such a horny little virgin, and I can't wait to give her just what she needs.

"Meet me in your window tonight," I grunt, turning to walk swiftly down the hallway before I say to hell with it, break down her door, and pop her sweet cherry right now.

———

Addy

Just as Alec said, Dad's having a dinner party tonight. Well, I've not been told officially, but a woman I've never met before is sent up to dress me in a long, flowing white gown that clings subtly to my curves and feels silky and luxurious against my skin. She helps me step into a pair of strappy heels before she bids me sit in front of the little white vanity in my room where she proceeds to curl my hair into soft waves that cascade down my back. I watch in wonder as she applies makeup to my face, somehow making me prettier without making it look like I'm wearing a lot of makeup.

She doesn't speak much English, and I can't help but wonder if that's by design. My father doesn't seem to want me to speak to anyone, although I still can't figure out why.

Suddenly, Alec's adamant instructions that I don't show any recognition toward him make more sense.

I'm still not entirely sure just what's going on, but I don't care anymore so long as it gets me out of here and in the same room as Alec, breathing the same air as him.

My heart skips a beat when I remember how he looked last night, naked in the moonlight, stroking that huge column of flesh just for me. When thick, white ropes shot from the tip, my body thrilled to its own climax, sweet release gushing from between my thighs.

Is it normal for me to want to feel his release on my skin?

My cheeks blush at the thought as I sit and stare at myself in the mirror. I don't recognize the girl—no, the woman—in front of me. I'm eighteen and officially a woman. The way Alec looks at me certainly makes me feel womanly.

I glance at my reflection again, taking in the slight shadow and mascara that makes my golden eyes pop. My lips are stained light pink to enhance their natural color.

Will Alec like what he sees?

I desperately want Alec to like the way I look. He's the only one I care about looking pretty for.

There's no knock at my door before my dad barges

in. I stand and turn to him, and his eyes widen for a fraction of a section before settling back into that fathomless expression I'm so used to.

"You look so much like your mother," he mutters.

I can't help it. I'm practically glowing with pride. It's the closest he's ever come to complimenting me. I know how much my mother meant to him and how much he still grieves her. So much so that he can't bear to look at me for my crime, and I bear my punishment without protest.

"Thank you," I murmur.

He frowns as if something doesn't sit well with him before he shakes his head and bids me follow him.

I do so, ever the obedient daughter.

When we reach the top of the staircase, he stops and turns to me. "I have several business associates I want you to meet. You may speak to them, but only speak if spoken to, and make sure you're the epitome of politeness. Do you understand?"

His voice isn't overly stern, but it brooks no argument.

"Yes."

He nods, seemingly pleased, before he places my hand on his suit-clad arm and leads me down the stairs. "Make me proud," he whispers near my ear before we come in sight of the guests mingling on the floor below.

All men. So many men. Just like that day long ago. The last day I was allowed out of my room.

Every eye turns to watch our entry, but there's only one pair of eyes I long to see.

My gaze sweeps the room before they finally find the forest, drawn to them like a magnet. He looks both hungry and pained all at once. I allow myself one moment to look before I tear my eyes away from Alec's, remembering how he cautioned me not to show any familiarity.

"Gentlemen," my father finally says as we near the bottom of the stairs, "I'd like you all to meet my pride and joy, our guest of honor for the evening, Addison."

I glance at him in surprise. His pride and joy? Guest of honor? I study his face, but I can't tell whether he's sincere or not. If I'm his pride and joy, why doesn't he ever come to see me or have anything to do with me? And guest of honor? Just what's going on?

Dad keeps me firmly by his side as he navigates us through the room, stopping to let different men talk to me.

Some of them remember me from that last dinner party I attended all those years ago, commenting on how much I've grown up. Something about the look in their eyes when they say that gives me pause.

Finally, we're standing in front of Alec, and I peek up at him in wonder, afraid to look at him full-on, afraid that my face will give away the depth of my adoration for this man.

"Alec, my daughter." Dad introduces me, although he doesn't extend the same courtesy to me. I don't care. I'm just grateful for an excuse to finally be near Alec

My head lifts to meet his gaze. I bite my lip when I finally see all the glorious shades of green in his eyes up close.

He shoots a passing glance at me before saying to my father, "She's just as pretty as you said, Jameson."

My heart plummets at the coolness of his tone. When a man next to us catches my father's attention, and he turns away for a split second, Alec's gaze instantly heats, reminding me of his true feelings and that this is all an act. But why? I still can't figure out exactly what's going on, though I sense that something isn't right.

I wish that I could move from my father's arm to Alec's. I wish I could walk with Alec, feel his touch, talk to him, just bask in his presence.

All too soon, Dad turns back around, excuses himself from Alec, and continues parading me around the room.

I chance a look over my shoulder at Alec to find his eyes pinned intently on me. They repeat what he whispered to me last night through my locked door.

I have a plan. I promise you that everything is going to be okay.

I force myself to turn away from him. I trust him. Whatever Alec has planned will make it so we can be together. He never explicitly said it, but his eyes do.

And that's what I trust.

six

. . .

Alec

I force myself to relax my grip around my glass before it shatters in my hand. I bring the liquid up to my lips and take a sip, trying to act natural and detached.

Fuck, it's hard, though, when the object of my obsession is being paraded around in front of a bunch of horny men—some of them older than her father. They're all eye-fucking her, imagining what she looks like under that snow-white dress. What they don't realize is that she is for my eyes only.

I'm the only one who's ever seen her completely naked, and I'm the only one who ever will. She entrusted me with that gift, and I'll do everything in my power to protect it.

I continue holding my drink in one hand and stuff the other in my suit pocket. I walk the room, nodding politely at the other men, stopping to make small talk with those who initiate it, all the while keeping a view on Addy out of the corner of my eye.

To the casual observer, I'm just another one of the unscrupulous businessmen here.

But I'm wearing a wire and circulating the room to capture enough evidence to take down this entire ring of criminals.

An old buddy of mine from college works for the FBI, and I called him up to get his advice on this entire situation with Addison. You'd think I'd resurrected his dead grandmother with how excited he was when he heard it was Donald Jameson I was trying to take down.

The FBI has been monitoring him and his ring of associates for a while now, but no one can ever get close enough to get enough dirt on them for any charges to stick. I'm now giving them that opportunity in exchange for Addy's safety. It's clear she's a victim of all this, and I just want her safe and free.

My instructions are simple. Capture as much audio feed as I can of their illegal business dealings, and preferably get evidence of Jameson attempting to auction his daughter off in exchange for business favors.

Sounds simple enough, but it's proving harder than expected with Jameson practically throwing his daughter to the wolves. For Christ's sake, these men are making no attempt to hide their lustful expressions as they leer at his *daughter*, and he's encouraging it. What the fuck is wrong with this man?

I'm practically vibrating with fury, my jaw tight. I have to get a hold of myself and relax, or I'm going to blow my entire cover. I take another sip of the amber liquid in my glass, not even tasting it as it glides across my tongue and down my throat.

I watch as Jameson prods his reluctant daughter, pushing her closer to an old man with thinning hair, a pot belly that his expensive suit can't cover, and a lewd grin on his face. The old man reaches out, placing a hand on the small of Addy's back, pulling her closer to him.

And I snap. I fucking snap.

I thought I could do this, but I was wrong. My vision turns red, and the next thing I know, my fist is connecting with the fucker's face.

There's a sickening crack as I break his nose, but I'm not fucking sorry at all.

I want to break much more than that.

"Garison! What the fuck, man?" Jameson screams,

his eyes hot with fury as one of his oldest business associates staggers back, screaming and clutching at his bloodied nose.

Before I get a chance to say anything, I see Jameson's eyes darken. I follow his gaze down to my shirt where my wire is clearly visible.

Fuck. He fucking knows I'm tapped. *Shit!*

My eyes flick to Addy's frightened face, her eyes big and round, her lips trembling in the face of such violence.

Jameson's mouth presses into a grim line as he reaches inside his jacket. His voice is eerily calm as he pulls the gun from his breast pocket and points it directly at me. "No one fucking betrays me—especially in my own goddamned home."

My only thought as I stare down the barrel of his gun is of Addy and what's going to happen to her if I die here tonight.

Before I can think beyond that or react, I hear the pop of the gun and a deafening scream from Addy.

I register the scene before me in slow motion. Addy's petrified eyes and perfect little mouth screaming "NO!" as she launches herself in front of me.

"Addy!" I shout as she falls to the ground, her arm covered in blood.

I fall to my knees beside her and frantically assess where the blood is pooling from her arm. I don't even register the chaos breaking loose around us as the FBI busts into the room, taking down Jameson and all these crooked assholes.

My only concern is Addison, my sweet, brave, innocent girl.

I locate where the blood is coming from, quickly removing my coat and tying it around her arm to staunch the flow. Thankfully, it only looks like a flesh wound.

Addy's face is pained and pale as she looks down at all the blood on her arm. "Alec…" She trembles, and I'm quick to soothe her.

I run a hand over her hair, noting vaguely how it's even softer than I imagined. "Ssh, it's okay. I'm here, baby. You're going to be just fine."

My chest tightens as I take in her tiny form sprawled out on the floor like a wounded bird. She took a bullet for me. She was willing to sacrifice her life to save mine. "Why did you do that, sweetheart?" My voice is hoarse with emotion. "You sweet, brave, stupid girl."

She doesn't hear me. Her eyelids flutter, and she passes out.

I gather her into my arms and cradle her to my chest. God knows how long I've yearned to have her in my embrace, but not like this. God, not like this.

My eyes dart across the scene of arrests being made to find my contact. "We need a doctor," I bark at him.

"Already got one on the way," he answers me solemnly, his mouth thinning into a grim line when he sees Addy in my arms.

"Jesus," he shakes his head. "How could a man do this to his own daughter?"

I don't answer. I just hug Addy closer to me protectively, silently vowing that Jameson will never get the chance to hurt her again.

Addy

The last thing I remember was Alec's gorgeous face and worried eyes looming over me, telling me that I was going to be okay.

When I awaken, it's Alec's face that I see again, although it's distorted and blurry. I blink, slowly, willing my eyes to come into focus.

I practically melt when his green eyes gaze into mine with relief.

I remember the gunshot and jumping in front of Alec. Oh, my god, my dad tried to kill Alec. But Alec saved me. He saved me from that creepy old man's touch. I can still remember the shudder that ran through me when I felt his hand on my back through my dress, the unsettling way he looked at me, the way my father pushed me toward him even though he could tell I didn't want to go.

I can still feel the sting in my arm, though it doesn't hurt nearly as bad as it did when the bullet hit me.

"Hey, baby," Alec croons, pulling me back to the present as he hovers over me, smoothing his hand over my hair.

I turn my face into his touch like an animal starved for affection, and I suppose I am. I can't remember the last time I was touched with such affection—if I've ever been.

I don't know where I'm at, but I don't care. I'm lying on a soft mattress, and I don't even take the time to look around the room. All I can do is stare into the green eyes that have captivated me since the moment I saw them through my window.

He leans down and places a kiss on both of my cheeks before he oh-so-gently presses his lips against mine. I instantly melt as a deep, soul-searing pleasure rockets throughout my entire body.

I kiss him back, pressing my lips firmly against his. I've never kissed anyone before, but Alec's lips on mine are beyond perfect for my first kiss. I don't know what I'm doing. All I know is what little I've read from romance novels. I want to taste him, so I act on instinct, opening my mouth and running my tongue along his lips. They're velvety soft, and a moan rises from within me.

Alec groans in response, his arms going around my back to hold me against his chest as he suddenly takes charge, pushing his tongue into my mouth.

And oh my god, the sensation of his tongue rubbing against mine makes my entire body feel weak. I'm like putty in his hands, melting into him as heat flares through me.

Alec alternates between dancing his tongue with mine and sucking on my bottom lip before he finally pulls back enough for us to catch our breath.

His eyes are hooded as I look up at him in awe. His breath fans over my lips, and all I want is more. More of him.

I boldly press my lips against his again, seeking more of his attention.

He kisses me before pulling away again with a groan, his expression tortured. "Addy, you just got shot. You need to rest, sweetheart."

But rest is the last thing on my mind. I'm finally with Alec. I'm finally out of my gilded cage, and I want to fly.

I shake my head stubbornly and bite my lip, nervous about being rejected. "All I need is you, Alec."

He stares at me intensely for a moment, looking

uncertain, before he finally seems to come to a decision.

"Fuck," he mutters before he smashes his lips against mine and kisses me savagely.

I bask in his kisses, my soul budding open, his for the taking.

I want nothing more than to stay in this man's arms forever.

I'm completely and irrevocably his.

seven

. . .

Alec

All I need is you, Alec.

Hearing those words from her sweet lips is my undoing.

"I can't deny you anything, sweetheart," I whisper to her in between kisses. I'm like a man possessed. I can't keep my lips off her now. I kiss her lips, her cheeks, her forehead before coming back to her lips again.

Her lips are like honey, and I'm a greedy bear hungering for more. I can't get enough. I'll never get enough.

"What do you want?" I whisper in her ear. "Just tell

me what you want, and I'll give it to you. I don't care what it is. It's yours." This tiny angel was willing to sacrifice her life for me. There's nothing I won't do for her. Nothing. If she says she wants me to give her the moon, you can bet your ass I'll find a way to do it.

After the shooting I brought her here to my place and had a doctor come by to check on her. There was no way in hell I was having her wake up in a cold, clinical hospital room.

The FBI has arrested her father and everyone else at that dinner party. Despite me snapping and not getting evidence of the planned auction, my contact told me that they should have enough to put them all away for good, especially considering how Jameson tried to murder me and ended up hitting his daughter instead. They can get him on both attempted homicide and aggravated assault charges, not to mention all the charges for the illegal business practices for which they now have evidence.

"You." Her husky little voice in my ear sends a tingle up my spine. "I want you, Alec."

"Fuck, Addy," I growl before taking her lips again. I pick her up and set her on my lap so that she's straddling me. She's still in her white evening gown, and it bunches up around her thighs as her legs part to settle on either side of me.

I hold her with both my hands pressed against her

tiny back. Fuck, she feels so breakable in my arms. So delicate. A surge of protectiveness wells up in me. *Mine.* Mine to love. Mine to protect.

She throws her arms around my shoulders and begins to move against me, rubbing her panty-clad pussy all over my hardness.

Fucking hell.

Her head falls back as she moans, exposing the long column of her neck.

I lean in and begin licking and sucking on it, feeling an excited tremor go through her when I taste the area behind her ear.

My balls are heavy and aching, and my cock is hard enough to bust concrete. I feel precum dribbling from my slit, staining the inside of my pants as she continues to hump me through our clothing.

How in the world did I get lucky enough to get this perfect, horny little virgin?

I groan and still her with a hand on her hip.

She whimpers and shoots me a desperate look, biting her lip in consternation. Her cheeks flush as she says meekly. "I'm sorry."

I give out a hoarse laugh. "Fuck no, baby. Don't be sorry. I love everything you're doing, but you've got to stop before I embarrass myself."

Her cheeks go even pinker, but she smiles up at me shyly, pleased by my response.

Fuck, she's so cute. I'm going to kill any mother-fucker who looks at her.

"Alec." God, I love the way she says my name. "I want," her blush deepens as she struggles to voice just what she wants. "I want…" she bites her lip, and I take pity on her, a pleased grin stretching across my face as my cock twitches underneath her.

"You want me inside you?" My voice comes out gravelly.

Her eyes flick up to mine before she nods shyly. "But I've never…" she trails off again.

"You've never had sex." My heart thrills at that thought. I love knowing that she'll be mine and only mine, that no one else has ever touched her and never will. "I know, sweetheart, and it's okay. I'm going to take care of you. You have nothing to be afraid of."

Her eyes search mine again before she nods. "I know that. I trust you."

My eyes settle on the bandage on her arm, and I frown. "Are you sure you're not in pain, baby?"

She shakes her head adamantly. "I'm okay. I promise. Please, Alec. I just want you." Her voice is bordering on desperation as she half pleads with me, and who am I to deny her?

I lean in and taste the honey of her lips again, allowing my hands to move over her supple little body, marveling at how responsive she is to my touch. She arches into me like a kitten, practically purring with satisfaction at each graze of my fingertips over her flesh.

I pull her dress up over her head, baring her naked tits to my hungry gaze.

I thought they were beautiful from a distance, but they're even more breathtaking up close. Rosy, pink tips stand out to me, just begging to be licked, and I happily oblige, bending over to suck one into my mouth as I swirl my tongue sensuously over the hard nub.

She moans and, as if she can't help herself, begins riding my hardness through my pants again.

I hiss when I feel her wetness seeping through her panties and my pants. Holy fuck, she's sopping wet. My mouth begins to salivate at the thought of tasting her, and I decide I can't wait any longer to sample what's mine.

I raise my head from her nipple and kiss her lips again as she works at the buttons on my shirt. I save us both some trouble and rip it off over my head.

I can't stop the swell of pride that courses through me when her eyes drop to my hard muscles, and her mouth falls open in awe. She leans in and presses her lips to my chest in a sweet kiss. I feel a strange lump in my throat at the sight. This precious fucking girl. She's everything. *Everything.*

"Lay back on the bed, baby," I tell her as I guide her down how I want her.

Her eyes never leave me as she watches me stand and shuck off my pants in one fluid motion, my swollen length bobbing free.

Her eyes widen as she takes me in, and she licks her lips before glancing up at me nervously. "It's so big, Alec."

I know what she's worried about, and I rush to soothe her fears. "I know, baby, but it'll fit. I promise you. You were made for me. You believe that, don't you?"

She nods as I crawl up onto the bed and settle my head right in between her legs.

She peers down at me questioningly, but my gaze is pulled from hers to the pinkest, ripest-looking pussy I've ever seen. It glistens with moisture, like morning dew on rose petals. I breathe in deeply, inhaling her intoxicating scent.

She trembles when I place my hands on her thighs, holding her open. "Alec…" she breathes my name and then jerks under my hands when I lick her.

"Oh, my god," she moans, her thighs jerking when I lick her again, paying particular attention to her pearly little clit. She's straining underneath me, her muscles tight as I hold her down.

"Relax, Addy," I breathe on her pussy.

She shivers as my breath fans across her sensitive flesh.

My cock is straining forward, begging for attention, but I ignore it for now. This isn't about me. This is about her. I'm dying to feel her orgasm on my tongue.

I continue to lick her in sure strokes, delighting in her little mewls and moans. She gasps when I finally suction onto her little nub and begin to press a finger inside her.

Her hands fly down to grip my hair as she begins to babble incoherently at me, "Alec! I...I...please...don't...I...oh, god!"

She's so tight I can barely fit one finger inside her. My cock is weeping a steady dribble of precum, jealous of my finger.

"Come on, baby. Let it go," I encourage her, knowing what she needs.

I suck hard on her little bundle of nerves one last time and move my finger in and out of her. Her fingers tug on my hair, creating tingles of pain in my scalp, but I don't give a fuck.

She releases a strangled cry. Her thighs shake, and I can feel her muscles quaking around my finger, milking it as her sweet juice floods onto my tongue.

She goes limp, and I can't wait any longer. I gather her into my arms and line myself up at her opening.

"Look at me, baby. I want to see those pretty eyes when I make you mine."

Her eyes snap open, still dazed from her release. I kiss her lips tenderly before I pull back and grip either side of her head gently, staring directly into her honey-colored orbs as I start to push slowly into her.

Her eyes widen at the sensation, and she whimpers, but she doesn't ask me to stop.

I'm pushing into her tortuously slowly, working myself through her tight muscles as gently as I can. I don't want to cause her any more pain than I have to, but I know it's going to hurt her when I break through her barrier.

If I ever get that far because, *fuck*, she's gripping my cock like a vise. Every muscle in my body strains as I fight the urge to slam into her.

Tight. She's so motherfucking tight.

She must see the torment in my eyes because she bites her lips and asks me, "Are you alright?"

I huff out a strangled sound. She's the one who took a bullet for me. I'm taking her virginity. She's the one who's going to be enduring yet more pain for me, and she asks me if I'm alright?

"Yes, baby," I manage to pant. "I'm just trying not to hurt you any more than I have to."

"I know there's going to be a bit of pain," she confesses to me. Her flushed cheeks let me know she's already feeling the discomfort of being stretched so fully. "Just get it over with, Alec. I can take it. I promise."

I search her eyes. "Are you sure, sweetheart?"

She nods, never breaking eye contact. "Yes, I want to be yours in every way."

Hearing those words from her lips, that she wants to be *mine*, is my undoing. Without further warning, I rear back and thrust hard.

I feel the tender flesh of her hymen give way under my invasion, and I'm suddenly gripped tighter than I've ever been in my entire life.

I hear her sharp cry, but her eyes never leave me, telling me that despite her pain, she's okay.

Jesus, if I thought she was tight before, it's nothing compared to now. Her inner walls are crushing me, sucking at me. She's hot and wet and pulsing all around me.

That coupled with our locked eyes is almost enough to make me come, but I force myself to hold back. I don't move a muscle because if I pump one time, I'll spill, and I don't want to do that. I want to savor this connection with her. I want to give her pleasure and feel her coming all over my dick when I fill her with my seed for the first time.

I didn't even ask her about condoms, and I'm glad she didn't say anything because although I've got some, there's no way in hell I'm ever having anything between us.

My chest is heaving up like I've run a marathon and sweat breaks out on my brow.

I lean down and kiss her, loving the way she arches her breasts up into me, rubbing her nipples against me.

"Fuck, baby, I could kiss you all day, but I need to make this good for you."

She mewls and wraps her arms around my neck, clinging to me.

"Yes, sweetheart. Hold on to me. I've got you. I've got you," I breathe into her ear as I pull out and then push back in.

We both groan in unison, and I feel the tiny ripples of her pussy vibrating around me.

"More, Alec," she pleads.

"Hot damn." I clench my teeth and pull out before thrusting in again. I continue that delicious dance until I'm pulling completely out of her and stabbing back inside, going deeper with each thrust.

The wet sounds of her tight channel sucking me in are more erotic than any porn film, and the way she arches up into me and bites her lip is every man's wet dream.

She's hot and horny and all mine.

"Mine, mine, mine," I chant with every jab of my cock. "Look at me," I pant at her when her eyes close.

Her eyes fly open.

"Whose are you, baby?"

"Yours," she purrs up at me, arching up into me again.

"Say my name," I groan, desperate to hear my name on her lips while I'm buried balls deep inside her.

"Alec," she pants.

I look down between our bodies, seeing her juices and blood on my girth as I continue to piston in and out of her tight hole. Mother*fuck*, the sight has my balls drawing up tight. I lick my thumb and rub it over her clit in small circles.

"Oh, god!" she moans.

I pump my hips harder and faster. She's right on the precipice, and I'm going to push her off it.

"Come on, baby. Come with me. You can do it. Give me that pussy."

She comes with a cry of my name, her back arching up off the bed and her pussy fluttering around me, falling open like a flower in bloom.

The feeling of my girl falling apart on my cock is too much, and I join her with a hoarse shout, my balls squeezing tight as they shoot my seed up my stalk to empty inside her in a glorious release of pure euphoria.

My cum explodes from my tip like a water hose, the pressure and release greater than anything I've ever felt before. After three jets, her pussy is swamped, but I keep coming. I can't fucking stop. I pump my hips again, trying to empty myself. My sticky cum drips out around my length, leaking down onto my balls and the bed. My entire body is tingling, and I'm surprised I don't pass the fuck out.

When I finally feel the last spurts drain from my swollen cock, I slump over her, barely catching myself on my elbows before I crush her.

I stay buried deep inside her, relishing in the aftershocks of her release. Her pussy is still tightening around me in little ripples as the waves of her orgasm subside.

Collapsing onto my side, I draw her up to me, kissing her and stroking my hands down her back, cradling her like she's the most precious thing in the world.

And she is. To me.

My Addy. My sweet little bird. I broke her out of her cage and set her free. And she chose to fly into my arms.

I'm the luckiest man on earth.

And the future is ours.

epilogue

. . .

Six Months Later

Addy

I bite my lip nervously as I wait for my husband to arrive. We may have only been together for six months, but we've been married for five. Call us crazy, but we both knew we were in love before we ever spoke a word to one another.

I loved Alec from the moment he saw me—*really* saw me. Him standing on his balcony and me painting in front of my window. I knew even then no one would ever make me feel the way he does. He's my knight in shining armor who rescued me from the castle.

He brought me out of the childhood home that was my prison, and I've never looked back.

It saddened me, of course, to find out what my father had been planning to do with me, but I can't say that I was too shocked by it. I never had a relationship with him, and now I never would since he's in prison for life, which he deserves judging by all the evidence the FBI gathered against him, thanks to Alec.

If I had to choose between my father and Alec, I'd choose Alec every single time. He was the first person ever to show me any love, and his love runs deep. I shudder to think of where I'd be right now if he hadn't moved in next door and found me.

Imagine my surprise to find out Alec grew up next door. All this time, he was right there, and I never knew. He didn't even know my dad had a daughter. I was a well-kept secret only divulged to potentially beneficial parties. It still hurts when I think about what my father did to me, how he convinced me my mother's death was my fault. Alec has made sure I know it's not, and I see that now. I'm coping and getting over everything. Thanks to Alec. Everything I have is thanks to him.

My life. My love. My freedom. My self.

Alec would give me the world if I asked for it. I know he would. But all I want is him.

And I plan on showing him just how true those words are tonight.

I'm already at the gallery, and I've ensured all the paintings are placed in the best lighting to highlight everything I want to capture.

I bite my lip again as I stare up at the biggest piece, hoping Alec will like it.

He should be here any minute. I booked a private viewing just for him before the exhibit opens to the public—a request the owner was more than happy to oblige.

I never thought I'd share my painting with the public. My paintings were always something I did to escape, but Alec convinced me how good they were. He returned to the house I was held captive in for so long, retrieved all my work, and showed them to an art dealer who instantly wanted to book me for an exhibit.

I'm nervous about sharing my work with the world, but with Alec by my side, I have the courage to do anything.

Speaking of Alec…

My breath catches in my throat when I see him. He'll always have that effect on me, I think. I love his broad shoulders, his broad chest, his strong legs, his stylishly disheveled hair. But most of all, I love his eyes.

Those eyes rescued me from my loneliness and gave me hope. Those eyes are my life. My everything.

And he's looking at me like I'm his everything, too.

He strides quickly across the room and kisses me. "Addy, baby, I missed you." His eyes finally move the painting I'm standing before. I step out of the way to offer him an unobstructed view.

My heart skips a beat as I watch him take it in, trying to read his expression. I see recognition, appreciation, wonder, and then humility.

"Addy," he whispers my name reverently.

I step up beside him and look up at my masterpiece, the painting I've worked so hard on.

It's his eyes. I've captured every color, but I've painted them with a forest in them. In the corner of one of them is a little brown bird, soaring free.

I know he'll understand the symbolism of the imagery.

He freed me and gave my soul wings.

"Do you like it?" I ask him timidly, needing his affirmation.

"It's incredible." The look he gives me contains so much love it brings tears to my eyes. "As are you," he adds as he draws me into his arms.

I never imagined I'd have this. This deep, soul-cleansing love.

"I wanted you to see how my heart sees you," I

explain to him. "You're my freedom. Your eyes saved me."

His throat works like he wants to say something, but then he finally grabs the nape of my neck and crushes his lips to mine. We kiss each other frantically, saying more with our lips than words ever could.

We don't need words. We never have. Our connection is deeper than that. It always has been.

Now for the second part of my gift to my husband.

He growls in protest when I break our kiss, but I ignore his attempts to pull me back into his arms, dropping to my knees before him instead.

I look up at him coyly as I unbuckle his belt.

"Fuck," he whispers as I pull his already fully hard cock from his pants. A deep vein runs up the side of it, and I run my tongue over it.

His swollen length jerks when my tongue reaches the tip, and a bead of moisture dribbles out of the slit.

I lick it up, swirling my tongue around his mushroom-shaped head.

His head falls back, and he fists his strong hands in my hair, though he's careful not to tug at my scalp.

That won't do. I want him to lose control.

Without warning, I swallow his entire length until the tip of him hits the back of my throat.

"Jesus!" he shouts, his grip tightening as he anchors himself in my hair, his hands shaking for control.

There. That's better.

I smile around his cock as I start to work him, bobbing my head up and down his hard length, making sure to get him nice and wet, and using my hands to fist his root that I can't fit in my mouth.

"Fuck, baby, stop!" he hisses at me.

I ignore him and keep going.

He lets out a guttural roar and jerks my head off him just as he starts to come.

Thick ropes fly out and land on my cheek before he yanks me up. He pushes my dress up and pulls my panties to the side with lightning-swift speed. I feel a rope of his sticky essence spurt out onto my thigh before he jams his still-coming cock inside me.

The sensation of his cum spurting inside me, filling me up, has me coming on him instantly. I'm half shocked. He didn't even have to stimulate my clit. That's how hot I got sucking him off and watching him come.

I let out a strangled gasp of my own as I thrust my ass back against him, grinding down onto him and milking out every second of our climax.

"Did you really think I was going to put this cum anywhere other than inside this sweet pussy where it belongs?" he rasps in my ear as he pushes his cock deep inside me and holds it there. I feel him still jetting inside me and mewl my appreciation as my pussy continues to quake around him.

"I want to breed this pretty little pussy," he says in between sucking on my neck. "Fill you up with my cum and watch that little belly swell with my child." Another spurt shoots out of him like just the thought made him come again.

"You won't have to wait long for that," I rasp, trying to catch my breath after the intensity of my orgasm.

He goes completely still before his arms tighten around me. He pulls out of me long enough to turn me around to face him.

His green eyes search mine, looking hopeful. "What are you saying, baby?"

I smile up at him. Time for the third part of my present. Alec has been trying to get me pregnant from day one. Every time we have sex, he makes comments about breeding me, and it turns both of us on like crazy. He wants to have a family with me, and I want that, too. Something I've never had. A family. And I just know it's going to be more than perfect with Alec. He'll be an amazing father.

"I'm pregnant," I say softly.

Pure joy lights up his face, and he somehow becomes even more handsome than usual.

He takes my face in both of his hands and kisses me deeply. "I love you, Addy," he whispers, his lips brushing against mine as he says the words I'll never tire of hearing.

"I love you, too, Alec," I throw my arms and legs around him just as he lifts me into his arms, seating his cock back inside me.

This. This is everything.

Alec helped me spread my wings and fly. He brought color to my life, and now everything is a beautiful shade of vibrant green.

I'm finally free to fly deep in his forest every day for the rest of our lives.

THE END

Connect with Emma!

Visit Emma's website to get a FREE book you can't get anywhere else: www.authoremmabray.com.